For Sophie and Louise Tanner

With thanks to Equipu plc

A Red Fox Book

Published by Random House Children's Books
20 Vauxhall Bridge Road, London SW1V 2SA

A division of Random House UK Ltd
London Melbourne Sydney Auckland
Johannesburg and agencies throughout the world

First published by Hutchinson Children's Books 1991

Red Fox edition 1993

Printed in China

RANDOM HOUSE UK Limited Reg. No. 954009

ISBN 0 09 918811 2

Watch Out For Fred!

Suzy-Jane Tanner

RED FOX

Ursulina and Frederika Brown are twins.
They start the day looking just the same.
They're never the same for long, though.
Fred always seems to get covered in whatever she is doing.

Like the time they were painting a picture for Mum.

'Watch out for Fred!' warned Dad.

As usual it was too late. Fred sat in the paintbox anyway.

Then there was the time Ursulina put on a ballet show
with her friends. Ursulina was Sleeping Beauty.
Fred *started out* as a sugar plum fairy.
But as usual she ended up as a monster.

'Watch out for Fred!' said Ursulina. The monster tripped over Sleeping Beauty on her way to ride her bike instead.

One morning the phone rang.

'It's Cousin Grizelda,' said Mum.

'She wants you to be bridesmaids at her wedding.'

'Goody!' cried Ursulina.

'Ugh!' gasped Fred.

'They'd be delighted,' announced Mum into the phone.

Mum took the twins to Bruin's Bridal Boutique
to hire the bridesmaids' dresses.
The dresses were pink and frilly.
'Don't they look sweet!' cooed the saleslady.
'Yuk!' said Fred.

'Watch out for Fred!' said Mum, as Fred chose a topper from the bottom of the pile.

'I hate pink!' muttered Fred.

The morning of the wedding arrived.
Mum washed Ursulina's fur first.
'Watch out for Fred!' called Mum, as Fred tried to escape.
Dad caught her just in time.

Fred hated having her fur washed.

Mum helped the twins put on their bridesmaids' dresses.
Ursulina sat nice and still.
'But it itches!' grumbled Fred.

Then it was Mum's turn.
She sat Ursulina and Fred on the bed so she could keep an eye on them.
Mum put on her prettiest dress.
She had a new hat too.

'Watch out for Fred!' reminded Dad, as Fred reached out to help Mum powder her nose.

At last everyone was ready to leave.
On the way to the car, Fred spotted an interesting-looking worm.
'Watch out for Fred!' yelled Dad. 'It's still muddy from last
night's rain.'

Mum and Dad marched either side of Fred down the path to the car.

They parked down the road from the church.
Fred wondered whether the engine oil needed checking.

'Watch out for Fred!' sighed Mum.
She stuck close to Fred all the way to the church.

The Browns waited by the door for Cousin Grizelda.
Family and friends had come from all over the world to be
at the wedding.

Ursulina kissed Grandma nicely.

Fred didn't want to be kissed at all.

She wriggled and squirmed, and got lipstick all over her face.

Fred was cleaned up just as Cousin Grizelda arrived.

After the wedding, it was time for the photographs.
'Smile please!' said the photographer.
'Watch out for Fred!' warned Dad, as Fred pulled her
best monster face instead.

Dad took Fred to stand right at the back.
There was a photograph of Cousin Grizelda throwing
her bouquet in the air. Ursulina caught it.

Then everyone lined up for a photograph together.
Ursulina stood right at the front with the bouquet.
She decided to do some ballet on her own.

Ursulina was so carried away with her pirouettes that
she didn't notice the big muddy puddle.
'Watch out for . . .

. . . Ursulina!'

SNAP went the camera.

It was Fred's favourite photograph.
They even printed it in the local paper.
Fred decided it wasn't so bad being a bridesmaid after all.

'Now I suppose we'll have to watch out for Fred *and* Ursulina!' sighed Mum.